no one
nowhere

E.S. HIGGINS

PEANUT PRINTS

No one, Nowhere
Their shadow is unevenly cast over the walls of the city
Shaping and curving over the lopsided bricks
The warmth of the sun is blocked out by the towers
That bring darkness and cold to all who are under them
They walk past a shop window
Their reflection is dirty and distorted
Unable to see, unable to hear, unable to listen
Drowned out by the ceaseless movements
along the road to nowhere.

There is an empire in the forest
Its majesty is in the trees
They sing in the wind

But to the ear that does not listen they creak.
They walk through the forest
Exhausted from the long journey
Their feet are sore and sweaty

And as they trek they pant from the effort
The trees breathe in their bad air
And return it to them fresh and new
They feel whole again

For a little while at least
Until they return to the city
To chase their shadows in the streets.

Growing up
Understanding
As time passes, things begin to make sense
A face emerges from the clouds
The sun warms it and it smiles
The storm is behind it
Gone for now but it still lingers
There is balance
A half and half of grief and joy
Grief over what has been
And joy for what is to come.

Looking into the darkness

Engulfed in silence

everything you carry with you shows itself

A private cinema

Of old smells and sounds

Like a broken record

The strings of your heart play

That song you made when you were a kid

Deep down you know you remember it.

There were three pigs in my living room one night

They danced in fishnets and high heels

I was sitting on the sofa, trying to eat dinner

But then the lights in the room started to float

They formed a ring around me

I was frozen in place, unable to move

Watching in silence as those pigs danced

They knew something about me

I could see it in their beady little eyes

They started to squeal

I panicked

The sound made me feel sick

They squealed as if they were in pain

Like they were scared

I was scared

I closed my eyes

Unable to take it anymore

I opened them again and the pigs were gone

I went to the bathroom

And looked at myself in the mirror.

When flowers bloom

And wilt

When people come

And go

Every moment is fourteen billion years in the

making

All of them have a purpose

Of coming and going.

STORM CYCLES

A hot midsummer's wind swept its way across the vast, brown fields. Nothing could be heard save for the gentle swooshing of the wind between the tall grass, and the distant rumbling of thunder from the approaching heat storm beyond the mountains. The sun was at its highest in the sky, but its light was rapidly being overtaken by the darkness of the clouds.

There was a town just a little way over from the dry fields. It was a small town – there couldn't have been more than a few dozen houses. Behind them stood the backdrop of an ancient and eroded mountain range. Not too long ago the town had been buzzing constantly with passers-by and exhausted travellers, but ever since the highway was built no one came through these parts much anymore.

The town had the feeling of somewhere that was no longer lived in. An empty shell of a place, where even the ghost of it had up and vanished. The people there were kind. Most of them had grown up in the town, and as the years went on they had children of their own, and many generations of the same family lived under one roof.

The storm was approaching now, and the gentle swooshing of the breeze turned into a howl. Old, rusted windmills span uncontrollably in the wind, too fast to even make their usual whining sound. People shut their windows and rushed into their gardens to rescue the washing, praying silently for the storm to pass once they were back inside.

The town was battered by the storm all night.

In the morning, the storm was over and the sun rose, just as it always had. The grass and the leaves were covered in droplets of dew, which shimmered like crystals in the rising light.

By midday, the sun had burned away all of the moisture, and the town was back to the way it had been before the storm. The rusty windmills groaned as they turned laboriously in the breeze, people opened their windows, and the distinct smell of freshly baked bread wafted down the empty, cracked road.

Jimmy Smith and his little boy Thebe walked into the field behind their house at midday. Jimmy had something he wanted to show his boy.

They made their way through the tall grass of the field, laughing and playing as they went. Jimmy had been a farmer before his injury. He was always a hard worker, working overtime most days, and sometimes well into the night and the early morning. He believed that life was made of hard work. He'd never experienced anything else until he had Thebe. Thebe opened him up to a world he'd never believed would be his. After the injury, Thebe was the one thing that got Jimmy up in the morning.

Finally, they reached the spot. It was a small, fertile patch of soil next to a small pond. Jimmy pulled out a handful of seeds from the linen bag he was carrying.

"Do you know what these are?" he asked Thebe, extending his palm so the boy could look at the four seeds that lay there.

Thebe shook his head. He was young and had never so much as set foot on a farm. The town had one small fruit and veg store. It wasn't much, but it was enough to supply the few families that lived there, even on their government benefits. Jimmy hadn't worked in over six years and solely relied on the dole. His income wasn't much, just enough to pay for food each week and to send Thebe to school.

Jimmy closed his palm again and dug a small hole into the soil before placing one of the seeds gently in.

"These are seeds. This is where life comes from. If you plant them under the ground like this—" he covered the seed with soil and patted it down softly "—and take care of them every day; make sure they're watered, and given enough sunlight, then one day a tree will grow."

Thebe's eyes widened.

Jimmy smiled. "This will be our tree. If we take care of it, no matter what happens we'll be together."

They kept that promise. Every week they came down and watered the soil.

It took many years for the tree to grow taller than both Thebe and Jimmy. A few years after that Jimmy passed away, leaving Thebe to care for the tree himself.

Thebe took the greatest care of the tree. It was everything to him. He'd sit under the tree for hours, reading, sleeping, and drawing. He missed his dad. Jimmy had been his best friend.

Growing up, Thebe had always dreamed of moving to Sydney. He had always felt alone in the small town. But now he felt he could never leave the tree. It was his responsibility, and more than that, he felt like he had a promise to keep to Jimmy.

Thebe was 24 when Jimmy died. His mother had died giving birth to him, so his father's death left him all by himself in a house large enough for a loving family. He got a job working at a nearby yeast factory. He hated it. The large industrial pumps and stirrers groaned all day and all night, so loud that Thebe couldn't even hear himself think. It made him miss the wide-open field with the tree in it, and the sounds of the wind rustling through the branches and leaves. It made him miss his dad.

He woke up one morning to see another storm was brewing over the mountains, as they rarely did . The townspeople prepared themselves for the worst. They boarded up their windows and covered up their cars. And for a time, it was as if everything was still. Suspended in time, the great inhale of a powerful storm seems to suck all the sound from the world. Sitting in his living room, all Thebe could hear was the ticking of the clock on the wall.

Not even the dogs barked.

But the storm ravaged through the town all night, and everyone was kept awake by the loud cracking and flashes of nearby lightning. Thebe lay awake all night, waiting patiently for the storm to end.

The next morning he went to the field. He fell to his knees in front of the tree. It was broken in half – the top half lay smouldering a few feet away, twisted and blackened by the lightning.

He sat there all day and didn't say a word. He sat there until the sun went down and the moon rose in its place. He sat there under the stars, and only left when he heard the distant screeches of the dingos making their way through the fields, and an unnerving rustle inside one of the bushes next to him that sounded like a snake.

He left the town the next day. He couldn't be there anymore. He couldn't stand the emptiness and the yeast factory. And now the tree that was once so dear to him and Jimmy was lying in ruin.

He hitchhiked all the way to the Sydney without looking back.

Thebe became a gardener and fell in love with one of his clients. They had a son he called Jimmy, after his father.

Years later, when little Jimmy was still a boy, he and Thebe returned to the old town. It stood there as it always had. His house was still there, but it was empty and overgrown by the vines in the garden. An empty shell of memories that felt lifetimes ago to Thebe.

They walked through the house together; it was damp but otherwise in good shape. Thebe stopped when he noticed the faded pencil marks on the kitchen doorframe. Dated lines of how tall he'd grown when he was a boy. He smiled with mixed emotions, and caught something deep in his throat that was trying to get out. He had never cried when his father died, and he wasn't about to now in front of his son.

He brought Jimmy to the same spot where his father had taken him. The tree was gone now, withered and ruined by the long years and weather. He took out a small linen sack full of seeds and showed them to Jimmy. And together they planted a seed where the old tree had been.

As they left the town they heard the distinct rumbling of thunder just beyond the mountain ranges, the first signs of the storm that would come.

Beauty is equal parts pain and happiness. When something is funny we laugh. When something is sad we cry. But when something is beautiful we do both. I remember when I held her again after all those years. We stood there laughing while tears rolled down our cheeks. Sometimes the most beautiful moments in life don't make any sense at all. We were in the middle of the supermarket when we saw each other. Everyone was looking at us like we were weirdos. But I didn't care. And I realised that my greatest dream and nightmare had come true. Love.

WIG OUT

"Get the fuck out of here and don't come back!" said the bouncer as he tossed a pair of skinny boys out of the club and into the cold back alley.

"Whatever bro, like we wanted to be in your shit club anyway!" yelled Macca. His and his friend Mitch's eyes were glazed and unfocused, a telltale sign that they were both severely fucked up.

"C'mon, bra, let's whip back at mine," said Mitch, grabbing Macca's shoulder and pulling him away from the wall of bouncers.

"Fuckin' oath we will!" Macca replied, stumbling over himself.

Before they left the alleyway, Macca spotted two girls walking past, and he stopped them. "Oi, where are you two hotties going?"

"None of your fucking business..." said one of the girls, a look of disgust on her face.

Mitch laughed, "Aw, come on, give us a smile, aye girls?"

The girls' disgust turned to revulsion, and before the boys could say anything else they stormed off.

"Ah fuck 'em… probably lesbian anyways," said Mitch. Macca laughed.

After a long journey with a lot of pit stops for resting and puking, the pair finally reached Mitch's house, which on a sober day would have only been a five-minute walk from the Sunken Ship – the shittest club in the whole area, but also their favourite.

"Can't believe the fuckin' dogs kicked us out, I'm not even that drunk!" said Macca as they sunk into Mitch's living-room couch.

"I dunno, man, I'm pretty fucked…" Mitch replied, sighing as his head flopped back onto the sofa.

Ever since they had finished school, Mitch and Macca had been a pair of delinquents. They had no aspirations, no skills (besides being able to withstand the most alcohol humanly possible) and their lives seemed to be going nowhere fast. They weren't fazed about it, they'd only just turned twenty. (Another thing they had in common was a shared birthday.) At school, they would always have to be separated from one another so classes could continue without interruption, and every lunchtime they wandered into the woods next to their school and punched out a couple of cones from the bong they had hidden there at the beginning of the school year. Their classmates from school remembered them as bullies, and although they made jokes at the expense of the other kids, and the teachers, they would have gladly received them in return. They were up for banter, and people that got to know them beyond the surface realised that they were just misunderstood.

"Should we get some girls over?" asked Mitch.

"I dunno, bra, do you know any?" replied Macca, and the two of them laughed for a while.

They sat around listening to techno for almost an hour until Mitch turned to Macca and said, "Dude, Brendon gave me a couple of acid tabs the other day that he had left over from his bush doof, you wanna try it?"

Macca paused for a second, he knew that he was pretty wasted already, but he didn't want to look like a pussy in front of Mitch, especially when it came to taking drugs.

"Yeah, man, let's fuckin' do it," said Macca, almost stoically, so Mitch got up and took a tin foil clump out of his fridge. He unravelled it and showed Macca two small tabs of acid that had pictures of cartoon characters on them.

"Brendo reckons you just stick 'em, under your tongue for a bit until they dissolve," said Mitch, passing Macca the tinfoil.

Macca took his tab and placed it under his tongue. The two of them were nervous, although they were both trying to hide their timidity from one another. Mitch said he'd seen a movie where the main characters took acid and listened to soul music, so he changed the playlist and the two of them sat back and waited patiently as the music played on Mitch's portable speaker.

Fifteen minutes passed.

"Fuck, bra, I'm bored already. Are you sure this shit's real?" asked Macca.

"Yeah, I think so... Brendon reckoned it was the strongest stuff he'd ever had."

"I hope so, I wanna see some dragons or something."

Twenty more minutes passed, before Macca, who'd been in the middle of retelling Mitch the story of when he got chased by some cops down at Manly, stopped dead.

"What's wrong, dude?" asked Mitch.

"I think it's hit..." Macca replied.

"How do you know?"

"I dunno... Everything just seems, brighter?" Macca sat back in his seat and zoned out, and after five more minutes Mitch felt the same thing.

"This is crazy…" said Mitch.

"Yeah, bra, tell me about it. I just lost myself for a bit there…"

"What do you mean?" asked Mitch.

"Close your eyes…"

Mitch closed his eyes, and in an instant, he felt like he was being sucked down a multicoloured tunnel at a million miles an hour. He felt and heard so much. There were so many voices, saying all different things that he couldn't quite make out, but he had a feeling that they were speaking words of love. He opened his eyes and looked at Macca. "Holy shit, dude…"

Macca wore the same expression on his face. "Fuck, man, I feel like I see you now."

"I know what you mean. I feel like I see everything now. It's like everything is connected. You and me. That's what I see, you and I are two parts of the same whole."

"Yeah, dude, I reckon if everyone took acid the world would be heaps better," said Macca, staring at his hands with a look of curiosity in his face. "My hands have the power to do anything I could think of… How fucked is that?" he continued, raising his hands to show Mitch.

"Yeah, I know, but what the fuck do we do with our hands but stupid shit? I feel bad

about those chicks we hounded tonight…"
Mitch replied.

"Yeah, bra, you're right… I feel bad too. I feel like if people were willing to put more time into getting to know me I wouldn't be such a fuckwit," said Macca.

"You're not a fuckwit, dude, you're my best friend," replied Mitch, putting his hand on Macca's shoulder.

"I wish I could express how I feel about the world. It's like I can feel it vibrating inside of me, I can see it in the wind through the trees outside, and I can hear it in the sound of a baby's laughter. It's everywhere, and I can't believe it took me till now to realise it all beats with one heart," said Macca, staring off into the corner of Mitch's living room.

"I know exactly what you mean!" exclaimed Mitch. "I feel bad about those girls tonight because in a way they are just extensions of myself, and disgusting them like that only made me feel disgusted in myself."

Macca stood up. "As of tomorrow I'm making a change, dude, I'm gonna read a book every week, and I'm gonna take that apprenticeship with my uncle."

Mitch stood up as well. "Fuck, yeah, dude! I'm gonna start studying, I'm gonna make an effort into putting out positive energy into the world, instead of the shit I've always done.

It always circles back to you, man, it always circles back…"

With their covenant, the two sat back down on the sofa excitedly, feeling as if they had just found the key to the world. But suddenly Macca grimaced.

"Are you good, man?" asked Mitch when he saw the expression on Macca's face.

"This is all too much for me right now, bra, I feel like I'm standing at the edge, looking down into some eternal abyss."

Mitch grabbed his hand firmly. "Just jump, man, I'll jump with you…"

The two of them closed their eyes and passed out.

It wasn't until late the next day when the pair awoke.

Mitch clutched his head, nursing a massive headache. "Fuck, dude, I feel so sick… What happened last night?"

Macca groaned and sat up slowly, wincing from the sunlight coming through the living-room windows. "Fuck knows, man, I don't remember shit…"

ENEMY IN PLAIN SIGHT

"Shut the fuck up, shut the fuck up!" Malaki screamed as he ran down the hallway. The power to the base camp had been cut, and now the only lights that guided his way were the emergency ones that lit the corridors with a sickly green glow. They didn't help much; in fact, they made Malaki feel more on edge.

They were here, of all places they were here.

Malaki burst through the landing door on the roof of the complex, still with his hands pressed firmly against his ears. He couldn't see his attackers, no one ever had. They came through the air, silent at first, but when their attack began the noise was unbearable. All of his friends were either captured or killed, and he didn't wait around to find out what his fate would be. But now he'd come to a dead end. He peered out over the edge, down to the ground twenty-four stories below.

He was a dead man either way, but he figured he'd rather take his own life than let them take him...

He looked at the sky. It was grey and stormy – a fitting backdrop. He looked back down towards the ground and swallowed.

"I'm sorry..."

Without another thought, he closed his eyes and jumped.

...

"You motherfucker!" yelled Captain Garth. Malaki gasped for air as he ripped the instrumentation and goggles off his face and body. He jumped up, frightened and disorientated for a moment. The simulations always felt so real.

He rubbed his eyes and looked at the captain. "How'd I go?"

Captain Garth shook his head. "Well, you survived the longest, but it was only because you left the others to die."

"What could I have done?" Malaki asked, innocently.

"You had multiple opportunities to save the others. When the attack first started you hid behind the weapons rack, and rather than help your fellow soldiers you grabbed yourself a pistol and made a run for it. When your friends were dying you never fired a shot, even though you were armed and able. If you weren't

Commander Skies' son I would have kicked you out a long time ago. You're a maggot, Malaki."

Malaki grinned. "Has the thought ever occurred to you that maybe I want to be kicked out? I have no interest in going to war. Guys with no future go to war, the ones with no ambition or no drive to make anything of themselves..."

"And yet they are braver and more honourable than you could ever hope to be," said the captain with distaste.

"There's nothing honourable about dying holding your guts in your arms while you cry out for your mother," said Malaki nonchalantly.

Captain Garth's face darkened, and Malaki could see the veins in his forehead throbbing. "Go back to base camp. I don't want to hear another word from you."

On his way back to base, Malaki was intercepted by one of Commander Skies' assistants, who told him that his father wanted to see him in his office. He sighed and followed the assistant to the other side of the camp, where the commander's office was located. They passed the muddy fields where initiates were crawling under barbed wire on their stomachs, the shooting range and the execution stand. Malaki looked at the empty noose that hung silently from the gallows, a constant reminder of the 'end of contract' agreement that he and the other initiates were held to if they decided to dash it before their three years' service was up.

Malaki found his father standing by the window. The commander turned around when he heard Malaki walk through the door. His face was fierce and regal, and when he motioned for Malaki to sit there wasn't a hint of a smile on his face.

"Do you know why I sent for you?" he asked.

Malaki sat up in his seat. He had no problems flaunting the authority of others, but his father's word was law, and it was a law that he was not willing to test. "I'm sorry sir, I don't know why," he replied.

Commander Skies shot back, "Have you not learned anything from your training? You were in that simulation for two months. I watched everything you did when the enemy came. You disappointed me."

"I'm sorry, sir," said Malaki.

"I don't want you to be sorry. I want you to be better. I want you to be a man. There's a war outside; whether you like it or not, you're going to have to fight."

Before he was able to stop himself, Malaki cried out, "But I don't want to fight! You all talk about this war, but no one has ever seen the enemy! How can I fight against something I've never seen?"

Commander Skies was silent. It was a silence so deep that Malaki felt like he could have fallen into it and never be found again.

"You want me to show you the enemy?" said the commander finally.

Malaki nodded silently.

"I hope for your sake that you're ready." Commander Skies opened up a drawer underneath his desk and pulled out a large, blank envelope. Wordlessly, he pulled out a stack of photographs and placed them on the desk in front of Malaki. "Look," he said, simply.

Malaki looked at the photographs. They were just pictures of pedestrians. There were large crowds of people walking on a busy sidewalk in the centre of a big city. People were waiting in line for their coffees, or boarding their morning bus to work.

"But, these are just pictures of regular people?" said Malaki, confused.

"There's nothing regular about them," said Commander Skies. "They're waking up. They're starting to question everything. Every command and every order they've been given, and soon they'll overrun us all."

Malaki sat back in disbelief. "But, I don't understand..."

"I never expected you to. You are young, and know nothing at all, even if you think you do. Do you know how this army works?"

"Loyalty, no surrender and companionship," Malaki began, but Commander Skies cut him off.

"Wrong again. This army is built on obedience. You obey your orders without a question, and then you might hope to understand something one day."

Commander Skies placed both hands on the desk and leaned over to look Malaki right in the eyes. "Get back in that simulation."

Malaki couldn't hold his father's gaze. Without another word he stood and left. He made his way back to the simulation room and opened the door. Captain Garth was still there, and he was still angry. "Motherfucker, I thought I told you I didn't want to see or hear from you again."

"Put me back in the simulation," said Malaki.

Captain Garth smiled. "Finally come to your senses then."

Malaki lay down on one of the many beds in the room and let the staff plug him in.

"Oh, and this time don't jump..." said Captain Garth, just before Malaki was put to sleep.

Malaki felt the plug slip into his neck and a moment later he sat up, gasping. He looked around the room; there were posters of half-naked girls and soccer teams stuck to the walls, and he guessed that he was back at his university dorm.

You never knew where the simulation would put you, all he knew was that this time he was ready.

This time when he was surrounded by the enemy he wouldn't run, he wouldn't jump either. He'd stand like a man and follow his orders.

DO YOU EVER GET TIRED OF LIFE?

It was Sunday afternoon when Quinten woke up. He covered his eyes and shrank from the light that beamed through the gaps in his curtains. The rays looked solid as they beamed through the dust and particles that floated around his room. His sheets were stained and damp-looking, and the dirty singlet he wore looked as if it had been cut from the same cloth.

When he finally rolled out of bed he stumbled over to the toilet and pissed. His aim was terrible, and a lot of it ended up on the floor. He shrugged and made a half-attempt at cleaning it up with some scrunched-up toilet paper.

Half an hour later he was driving to work. It was a miracle he made it without crashing – he fell asleep almost every time he drove, and by some stroke of luck would always wake up at the last moment. A part of him wished he wouldn't.

He parked outside of work and attempted in vain to tuck his shirt in, but it ended up looking scruffier than if he'd just left it out. He was good at his job. He'd been working at the supermarket since he was fifteen. He was forty-five now. Things had changed a lot since he started. Working at the supermarket used to be fun for him, but over the years it became so legislated by the higher ups, that it was hard for him to do anything besides work. He'd take naps whenever he could, but even that was harder these days now that he was the night-fill captain. Five in the evening till one in the morning, sometimes later. That had been his shift six days a week for the last thirty-odd years.

His friends used to ask him if he ever got tired of working at the supermarket. He'd always shrug and say, "I dunno, you ever get tired of life?"

He clocked in and got to work. There was a lot of stock to fill the shelves with tonight. He didn't mind it, he'd gotten so used to the work that he'd go into autopilot and daydream the whole time. He'd think of random stuff. His thoughts never had patterns. Sometimes his daydreams turned into elaborate stories, where he'd end up doing something crazy like hijacking a plane or jumping off of a building to escape zombies. The lights in the supermarket were a sterile white, and combined with the white floor, would sometimes make him imagine he was walking down the corridor of a hospital.

Hours went by as he stacked food onto the shelves piece by piece. He opened box after box and threw the empties into the trolley he brought with him.

His shift ended and he drove home in the dark, falling asleep more than once and waking up every time.

He walked into his room, took his clothes off and looked at himself in the mirror in silence for a while. He was out of shape and hairy; he was bald, and the bags under his eyes made him look as if he'd been in a fight and lost.

He sighed.

The next day he woke up with a groan and went to work. And then the next day, and the next after that.

That was how the years went by. A constant cycle of falling asleep and waking up, and then falling asleep again. More years went by, and he still woke up groaning.

Five years passed the same. One early afternoon, he awoke as usual. His alarm buzzed on his bedside table, and he rolled over onto his face. Twenty minutes later he left for work. The drive from his place to the supermarket was half an hour or so. It took him through the windy roads in the state forest and past the lagoon before he finally popped out at the road behind the supermarket. It was a strange and swampy forest that had inspired a lot of local legends and superstitions. Most people that lived around the forest believed beyond doubt that there were ghosts along the road that wound through it. The most common story was of a woman in a white dress who appeared in the back seat of people's cars and made them crash. Quinten didn't believe the tales, but nevertheless he always felt wary driving back through the dark forest after work. He was tired today. More tired than he had ever been. It wasn't for lack of sleep, but lack of life. At last, after all those years, he began to feel dread and resentment towards his job at the supermarket. More and more often he found himself swallowing his regrets as he worked in silence. And, to his dismay, the more he pondered on his regrets, the more regrets he seemed to find. He got out of bed and picked his work clothes off the floor. Twenty minutes later he was winding down the state forest road sleepily.

It was midwinter, and after turning the heat up in his car Quinten began to feel very comfortable. Slowly his eyelids closed, and he lurched them open again. There was a brief battle against the sleep that sat heavily atop his eyelids. But ultimately the battle was lost, and he drifted away. He did this most days. Usually, he'd be asleep for only a second or two before one of his wheels went over the bumpy lines that barred the edge of the road, and he was vibrated awake again. But this time he kept sleeping, and a moment later he spun off the road and crashed the car into a tree. He lifted his face from the airbag, dazed and confused, but unhurt. A few moments later he realised what had happened. His car was wrecked. His phone was wrecked in the crash too, and no cars came by for almost half an hour. He looked at his watch – the glass face was cracked, but the hands still ticked. He knew he'd be late if he waited for cars any longer, so he decided to walk the rest of the way.

When he thought he was close enough to the supermarket he tried to cut through the trees to save some time. He squelched through long grass and tore through tall plants and bushes. Grey clouds amassed behind him, and soon the forest grew dark. A few minutes later thunder clapped over the hill, and then it started to rain. It poured from the heavens, so heavily that it was hard for him to see. He winced as he rushed through the trees. He was too far through his walk to turn back, so he pushed onwards. His feet got soaked as he trudged through muddy puddles, and soon he was up to his knees in water. He started to panic. His clothes were soaked through and heavy on his back.

The rain got heavier and heavier; it was hard for him to breathe. It was too deep now to walk or even wade. The water had risen about him so suddenly that his only option was to swim. He was never a good swimmer. He swam as hard as he could, but it was as if he was swimming against jets in a pool. Great streams of rainwater rushed down the hill behind him, and after a small but intense effort, he tired out and just managed to grab hold of a thick tree branch before he was swept away. He looked downstream at the enormous waterfall that had formed. The roaring of crashing water deafened even the sounds of thunder and lightning above him. For the first time in his life, Quinten wanted nothing more than to live. The fear of dying was what made him wrap his arms tightly around the tree branch, and it was the willingness to live that held them there. But it felt too late. The water level was rapidly rising, and a few moments later the branch that Quinten clung to snapped.

He yelled and tried madly to swim towards another, but the current was too strong. It pulled and pulled and pulled, and the muddy, grungy water rushed over the edge in front of him and obliterated into vapour below. Suddenly, he gave up swimming, as if even the will to live had been washed away from him. He let the rushing water grasp him and pull him towards the edge, and as he fell he closed his eyes and waited to be destroyed.

For a few moments, he dropped and felt butterflies in his stomach as he plummeted into the darkness. And he was happy.

WATERFALL

One of the greatest realisations a person can
have is when they realise they are at one with
the world. Energy flows like water, and over
time it carves deep gorges through even the
hardest rock. Even the hardest of souls is
broken into its essence one day and swept away
by energy.

A man sat next to a waterfall that was
deep within a forest. He'd been there for longer
than he could remember, listening, watching
and waiting. He hadn't spoken for so long that
he'd forgotten the sound of his voice, and he
doubted anything would come out if he'd tried
to say anything anyway. He didn't need to
speak; there was no one to talk to, save for
himself. He sat there watching the wall of water
rush down in front of him, and through its
stream he could just make out the reflection of
his distorted face staring back. He had lived in
the city once, but that was many years ago. In
those days, he felt twisted and disconnected
from his body, like a puppet with multiple
puppeteers all pulling at different strings. He

walked around stiff-backed and stressed all the time, stuck in a suit that fit him snugly but chafed his soul every day. Repetition upon repetition had worked to turn his life into an existential blur. That world was no longer his. One day he snapped. He lost control in public and nearly beat someone to death. He'd never been a violent person; he guessed it was the years of frustration finally coming to a tipping point. For a long time afterwards all he felt was shame. Shame for what he had become. At the time it felt right, almost cathartic to let all of his anger and frustrations out on someone else. But that was blind rage. That unfortunate person was just like he was.

He left the city behind, along with everything that he owned, although that wasn't much. He had no family to say goodbye to, and no friends who would miss him. For years he'd dreamed of living in the forest. It was his favourite thing to think about when he had the time. On weekends, he often stayed in the forest overnight, or did wilderness survival courses. At night, he studied plants and natural medicines, agriculture and hunting tactics. When the time came for him to finally enter the forest on the outskirts of the city, he never came out again. Over time he learned what plants to eat and where to find food. He learned what plants to avoid, which could heal him from pain and help heal him from sickness, and after much searching he came across the waterfall, where he'd sat ever since.

But that was a long time ago, and he felt old now. His beard had grown out over the years, and now it rested in his lap when he sat. His hair was long and matted, and his face was bronzed from the sun and hardened. He thought much over the years, so much that his mind was emptied save for the echoes of birdsong and the crashing of the waterfall. Not for a minute had he ever regretted leaving the city behind and journeying into the forest alone. In fact, he never felt alone in the forest. And although he sat in silence, all around him was the ceaseless beating of life. The birds sang in the sunlight, and the sounds of the crashing waterfall echoed through the forest day and night, and even when he was off gathering food he could hear it calling him back. Those were welcomed sounds, much more than the engines of cars or the horns of big trucks passing through the streets in the night. Those sounds were designed to push people away, never to bring them closer.

The high sun and the shadows of the trees guided him through the forest during the day, and in the evenings, he was guided through the darkness by the stars in the sky. Whenever he was fed and didn't need to hunt at night, he lay on his back and peered up at the stars, and listened to their music. He'd done much thinking since he'd sat by that waterfall, and at the same time none at all. He'd come to the conclusion that nothing he did or thought would matter in the end.

Years passed by and still he watched the water fall and crash.

One morning he stared into his reflection, and without thinking he dipped his hand into the water slowly, and when he pulled it out again it was gone. His hand had disappeared completely. He wasn't in pain, and after inspecting his handless arm for a moment he smiled. With great effort, he lifted himself onto his legs and moved silently into the water, and was washed away. The birds sang and the crashing of the waterfall echoed through the forest, just as it always had, and always would.

CHARACTER

Deep in the countryside of northern New South
Wales Rob sped down a long, straight highway
in an old rusted Holden Commodore. The soil
was red, and the grass was a yellowy-brown
colour, which looked beautiful in the sunshine
but was the result of long months of the tough
drought that was so common in Australia.

Far off into the distance, he could just
make out the mines that stood like giant anthills
on the horizon. Every person that saw them was
left with mixed emotions; both appreciation for
the ingenuity of humans but also a grim insight
into their destructive nature.

The Commodore slowed down and
turned onto a dirt road that led downwards
another kilometre or so into the chicken farm
Rob worked at.

Rob hadn't always been a country boy.
At thirty-three, he had grown tired of the
bustling streets of Sydney, and a week after his
girlfriend left him he decided to pack up his
things and move. He had been a writer, trying
to make it in the film industry, but after many
failed attempts he had given up and resigned

himself to the fact that he probably never would have made it anyway.

Moving to the country was a tough adjustment at first, but in time he fell in love with the land. He loved the quietness of the fields and the cool breeze that swept over the grassy plains each morning and evening. He felt at home there.

Rob got the job at the chicken farm purely by chance. He got into a conversation with an old boy called Greg at the local pub, and after a couple of rounds, Greg offered him a job working as a farmhand on his chicken farm just outside of town.

Rob took it, and soon after that he moved into an old shed out the back of the farm. It wasn't luxurious, that's for sure, but Rob found it hard to complain. Every morning he'd stick his head out with a cup of tea and drink it whilst he gazed out at the mountains on the horizon.

He respected Greg, too. Although Greg was the embodiment of every negative country stereotype that Rob had heard of in the city, he could only be thankful for Greg's generosity and his honest compassion. Greg was rough, vulgar, and downright disgusting sometimes. But he was honest. Behind all the grit and grime, he was the most compassionate man Rob had ever met; he just showed it in different ways. Greg's type of compassion was given through insults. The more he insulted you, the more he liked you. Greg would always make fun of Rob for his soft hands, or his lack of coordination when it came to anything manual, but he respected him because he worked hard. Rob became so close to Greg and his family that he'd often babysit Greg's grandchildren.

On one of these occasions, Greg came home at eleven thirty to find his grandson Mitchell still awake in bed. He confronted Rob, but Rob was adamant that he'd sent Mitchell to bed at eight o'clock, to which Greg replied, "Sent to bed? Well, you've obviously not tucked him in and read him a story! No wonder he's still awake, ya fuckin' idiot!"

He turned to around to Mitchell and began tucking him in. "Come on, time for sleep, ya little shit."

Mitchell smiled and yawned sleepily. "I love you, pop."

Greg smiled and kissed Mitchell on the forehead. "Yeah, I love you too."

On Friday afternoons, Rob and Greg would sit on the back of Greg's ute and drink beers until the sun went down. They'd talk about all sorts of things – girls, life, the city, and family. Greg's son was in prison for armed robbery, and ever since Greg and his wife Lola had taken care of his kids.

One night they were on the topic of people, and Rob was saying that, even though there were a lot of bad people in the world, they all had some good in them. He believed that everyone could be changed.

Greg laughed, "Fuck me, I remember when I used to think like that. I've been alive a lot longer than you have, and I've met a whole lot of people. I realized a long time ago that some of them were just cunts."

The two of them laughed and Rob made his rebuttal. "But I'm sure if you just took the time to get to know them, you'd see some good in them."

Greg shook his head, "Me best mate's one of the biggest cunts I know… And what? You reckon you're better than them that you can see the good in them? You're just a cunt like the rest of us!"

They laughed together as the sun dipped beneath the mountains on the horizon, and twilight fell upon the countryside.

A few more months passed, and Rob had never felt happier. All around him was the poetry of existence, and he'd never been more inspired to write. He wrote every night, and often right through to the early mornings too. There was a fire in him that he'd never felt before, and every day it seemed to grow inside of him. After every breath he took he exhaled poetic energy, and everywhere he looked he was met with beauty beyond words.

He knew then that he had to go back to Sydney. It all made sense in his head; he would write poetry. He would start on the streets first and write poems for anyone that he talked to, and from there he'd write books and sell them on the side. There was something in him that he felt deep down, a surety of his path, and he knew that this time he would make it.

In one of his poetic moods, he revealed his plans to Greg, who laughed and said, "You're not fuckin' gay, are ya?" before winking cheekily.

Not long after the day came when it was time for Rob to leave. Greg, Lola and their grandson stood by Rob's rusty Commodore, waiting for him to stuff the last of his bags into the car. He turned and hugged Lola and Mitchell before stopping in front of Greg and putting his hand out. Greg brushed it away. "Fuck off, mate, give us a hug."

The two of them hugged goodbye, then Rob finally hopped into his rusty car and sped off down the dirt road towards the highway, disappearing behind a thick cloud of red dust.

Rob drove down the old highway, staring out into the dry yellow countryside, and when he finally passed an old, faded, green road sign that pointed towards Sydney he smiled to himself.

LOVE SONG

You always used to talk about Portuguese tarts
I never even told you that I liked your art
I was head over heels from the start
And afterwards I always wondered why
You said goodbye
And I'm still in love with you
But all I've got are memories
Memories,
Of you

I was young it's no fault of mine
If I had another chance at love I'd try
But it takes a lot of loving to turn darkness to
light
It's funny then that I only think of you at night
And when my head is resting on my pillow
I close my eyes and think of you
But now I'm a world away
Haven't seen you in a lot of years
I still remember how I shed all those tears
But now I understand and I'm only thankful
Of you

And now all I got are memories

Memories of you
You're still out there but I'm not sure where
A part of me wishes that I didn't care
Staring out the window when I'm on the bus
Watching the hands tick over on my watch
Seconds further away from when we were
And now all I've got are memories
Of you

A very odd and inconvenient thing happened to Mr Adams one morning on his stroll to work. He died.

Think of change in your life like you would a flower blooming. If you stare at a flower bud waiting for it to bloom, you'll drive yourself crazy waiting. But if you were to film it and watch it again on time lapse, it would look as if the bud was bursting into life. Change happens slowly, but every moment is still changing from one to the next. Our journeys are slow. But if you make a story out of your life, and fill it with ups and downs, losses and gains – at the end of it all you'll have something beautiful and full-cycled. The most beautiful things in life are part of a cycle. The flower wilts and dies after a short while, and the cycle starts again. The same as when everything you've gained is lost. It fills you with feelings of bitterness and spite. Sometimes you hate the world and everything that's happened to you. You could wander the world feeling utterly lost for years, hollowed out and desperately trying to find your way again. Time feels like it moves slowly in those periods of our lives. But every step you take is one closer to the realisation of your inner story. And if you sped up your life, just as you would a flower in a time-lapse, you'd see that you're on your way to blooming again.

A moment of silence in a dancing crowd

You stare into space and lose the sound

You're somewhere else, nowhere to be found

Although you feel safe, all your friends are around

As you float away by yourself for a while

You look at all the dancing people and smile

Moments like that don't last forever

Moments like that I pray I remember

When tomorrow comes.

NOTES FROM THE BUS

All we can really do at the end of the day is make a choice out of the limited knowledge we have and pray that it's the right one.

Death doesn't seem so bad if you believe in something.

All I want from life is to one day understand something.

An artist sees their life as a blank canvas. A writer sees theirs as an empty page. To be the embodiment of your craft is the ultimate goal.

One day even the tallest mountains will fade away like dust in the wind.

Everything has its place. Even you.

You still get growing pains as an adult, but now they're all internal.

And everyone who lives one day fades away like words in the sand

And they leave holes in our hearts although we still can

Visit them in our memories; they live on forever there

Their words and energies live on through the blessings you share

The gift in life is that we all live it together

Daytime and nighttime and every weather

So live on for those after you and before

And accept that a day will come when we won't be anymore.

When something is funny, we laugh,

When something is sad, we cry,

But when something is beautiful, we do both.

Years after the human world ended, the vines had crawled out from under the abandoned buildings

Pillars of dusty light beamed in through their dirty and broken windows

There was nothing but memories left

Shadows of a time that once was but never would be again

Wind rushed through the empty hallways of the buildings

Slamming and opening doors like a great orchestra

Nature had almost forgotten the touch of humans

Every day it was reclaiming everything that had been taken from it

And on that day when the work was complete

All things would be at balance.

Life is just a messy canvas covered in paint

The harder it gets the longer you wait

To take a chance, although that's what life is for

To do the next day what you couldn't before

And how it ends doesn't matter because all things become art

As long as you're willing to take a chance and start

What are you waiting for?

There's an empty chair that sits under a soft light

An old man used to sit there but now he's gone

No one has sat there since and now it stands alone

Waiting to be sat on

You pass by and notice it there

And the sight intrigues you deeply

You wonder where the old man went

And although you think of the obvious, a part of you knows he's still out there somewhere

You wonder if he misses his chair

Sometimes that's all we think of during long journeys

Our favourite chair or the softness of our own beds

Things to look forward to on the road to nowhere

The light coming through the window in the morning

The wind rattling against it in a big storm

The heat and steam from a nice warm shower

Stretching your legs out in bed after a long and tiring day

I wonder if the old man still does all those things

I don't know his name or I would ask him

I wonder where he went

And I wonder when he'll be back to sit on his chair again

Along the road to nowhere.

Change is what you make it

Love is how you take it

And return it to things that need it most

Health is how you keep it

The food and how you eat it

That feeds your body and soul

Knowing is in the action

The heart and its reactions

The power to make you whole

The mind is how you perceive things

Regardless of how you see things

What you reap is what you sow.

There's a fly caught in a web on the windowpane

And the spider's moving closer and closer

It beats its wings faster, but it's caught in a trap too strong to break

I go to free it before the spider comes

But my finger stops before I break the web

If I free the fly the spider dies

And just like that I disturb the ebb

And flow, those decisions could never be mine

For just as the spider consumes the fly

It too gets consumed in time.

Looking at yourself through the ripples in the water

You reach your finger down and connect

You seem different there

Vapours of a memory

Of a time that's gone but will stay with you forever

The memory brings an intense yearning in your heart

For a time when all was safe and sound

You're still alive there

It's not you anymore but who you were

You meet eyes for a moment

But they look away

You were never meant to make contact

Only to observe

So, you watch in silence until the ripples fade away.

PLANS RUINED

It was just like any other rainy morning when Mr. Klaps went for his daily stroll. He wore a long, chequered overcoat, and he had a moustache that he twisted at the edges. His walk was stiff and straight, and when he turned to look at something he used his whole back as if he had no neck at all.

For twenty years he'd woken up early and gone for his walk. It became such a ritual in his life that he found he couldn't seem to function properly throughout the day if he missed it. The walk would take him across his street, through the park, and out again into a row of little cafes and bookstores. Under his arm, he held the daily newspaper close to his chest, and above him, he held his small, black umbrella to keep off the drizzle that pattered against its canvas.

In fact, Mr. Klap had become so enmeshed in his daily rituals that he became distrustful of anything that sought to interrupt them. When he had to go to breakfasts with family, or see friends, when he was away on business, or worse, ill, he thought always and only of his little walk. It was where he felt most like himself, grand and noble. He breathed in the fresh air from the flowers in the park, and walked with considerable grace over the asphalt footpath, scowling at joggers who ran by him too closely.

As he walked he flipped open the newspaper of the day and analysed the front page.
But after only a few short moments, he scoffed to himself and folded it up once more. Mr. Klaps had subscribed to the local newspaper for twenty years, and not once in that time had he ever made it past the front page. But even though he scoffed at it, sneered and sometimes groaned, it was still a vital part of his daily ritual and one that he was not ready to let go of.

The clouds were dark and grey, heralds of the long winter that would follow. But Mr. Klaps didn't mind. He loved the rain. He loved its fresh and sweet smell, and he loved the coolness of the breeze that carried the moisture. What he loved most were the first moments where sunlight burst through the clouds and ignited droplets of rain that hung from trees, benches and houses. They glimmered like crystals in the light. And for a brief time, Mr. Klaps felt a sort of happy melancholy. A sight that we understand is beautiful makes us happy, but we're saddened that we could never know why. Those things just are, and Mr. Klaps was happy to keep them that way.

When he was halfway across the park a little boy approached Mr. Klaps on the footpath. Mr. Klaps eyed him distrustfully. He had a quiet resentment towards children. There was something about them that put him on edge. It was like they knew something about him that he didn't, as if their innocence was a conduit for some strange energy that gave them foresight.

He tried to step around the child but as soon as he did the boy moved to block the way.

"Hi!" he said, grinning as he waved up at Mr. Klaps.

Mr. Klaps paused for a moment before dipping his hat seriously. "Good day." Mr. Klaps breathed relief; he had been expecting worse than a friendly hello, but children always had a way of surprising him. He went to pass the child again, but again the little boy moved and stood in his way.

"I've said hello to you, now run away before I get very cross!" he scowled at the boy.

The boy shook his head sweetly. "Only if you come and see my special tree!"

"Out of the question," snapped Mr. Klaps, but before he had a chance to step around the boy again, the little boy grabbed his newspaper and ran towards a large tree that stood twenty metres away.

"You little...!" Mr. Klaps roared as he took off in an awkward power walk. He hated running, especially if it was after something. He was livid. His ritual had been soiled already by the boy, but now that he had run off with his newspaper the morning was ruined beyond repair.

He reached the tree and circled it. The boy was nowhere to be seen. But on closer inspection, Mr. Klaps realised that the tree was hollow. There was a tight opening in the tree, just large enough for him to squeeze through. He poked his head in and looked around. The little boy was in there; he could feel his presence.

Mr. Klaps squeezed clumsily through the opening and was shocked to find himself falling. He yelled as he plummeted down and down further into the darkness. His hat flew off, and his little black umbrella twisted inside out above his head.

He fell for what seemed like an eternity until he landed softly in a bed of flowers. He looked around in disbelief at the giant mushrooms that grew multicoloured around him. And all was silent, save for a little stream that trickled past Mr. Klaps's hand.

He saw the little boy there, smiling at him toothily. "Where are we?" he asked, timidly.

The little boy giggled. "Nowhere."

WINDOWS TO THE SOUL

An old man looked at himself in the mirror one evening. He stood in silence while he studied his face. His skin was wrinkly and covered in liver spots, and his hands were puffy and soft. He looked at the wisps of hair on his head and the scars on his arms. Memories of times that once were but would never be again.

He could barely recognise himself from what he used to be, and he looked very different to how he felt inside. His eyes were the only things that remained of his old self, dark brown and intense. He wondered if someone were to see only his eyes how old they would think he was. He had the eyes of a twenty-five-year-old, and the body of a man who'd lived longer than he should have. He was constantly battling with his body. On days when he wanted to explore, his legs were too tired and sore to leave his chair. His shit often came precisely when he didn't want it to, even though he'd sometimes spend over an hour on the toilet with no success. It was a strange idea to him that he could lose control of his body.

It made him wonder if it was ever who he was. He wondered if his soul would still be there when he died, looking over his cold, stiff corpse with everyone else in the room. His only vessel to communicate with the physical world. He wondered what he would do when that day came. Would he be in denial? Would he haunt the old places and people in his life, trying desperately to grab their attention, for them to see and to know that he existed and was crying out to them? He wondered if he'd join the great oneness of the universe, or if his essence would join the stars. He wondered if his experience and emotions would float in the ether, waiting there for another to borrow and forge into music and art. He wondered if people would hear him in the laughter of babies or the wind through the trees. And then the thought that there could be nothing at all dawned on him.

He thought of nothingness.

He thought of darkness and a neverending, deafening space.

He'd often heard people saying nothing happened after death. He wasn't a religious man, but he always had trouble agreeing. They seemed so convinced that when we died there was nothing. But when he asked them to describe life they couldn't. He would ask them how, then, if we can't describe what life is, or why it started, how could we know what death is?

He was ready for death. His body only weighed him down now, and he was eager for the journey.

He just hoped that people would remember his eyes.

When you die do you float above your body?

You wonder if it was really you at all

You look at yourself in the reflection

You are nothing now but a calm breeze and some wisp

Floating across the world you travel far and wide

Only to find yourself back where you started

A flower is growing on your grave.

LITTLE FEET

Wind chimes sang a lonely song upon the porch on a windy day. A mother was in the garden hanging up laundry. The house was made from wood and was only one story. A modest, but cosy home filled with old trinkets and things that no longer worked.

Her days were spent listening to the wind chimes, her only company in the lonely house. There had been a time when she couldn't hear the wind chimes at all. When her children were growing up. They'd run around the house and bang into walls. Doors would swing open and slam shut and the sound of little feet running across the wooden floors would vibrate through the house. There were three of them. A little girl and two boys.

She loved her children more than anything in the world. She wished they'd come and visit her more. For most of her adult life, her thoughts were only of her children. Of where they were, or if they'd eaten, how they were going in school, and when she needed to take them to soccer games. And now that they were all gone she wondered the same things, but it was her that needed to be taken care of, to be comforted and hugged. A hug is when two hearts combine briefly as one when two people share one body. The distance between two people after a hug is called longing, and the emotion when that hug can never be again is called pain. She had felt a lot of pain over her life.

Every afternoon, she walked through the fields next to the house. She picked flowers and put them into a little woven basket to take home and use to decorate with.

The clouds on the horizon melted into the mountains and the sound of a distant waterfall echoed over the fields. Sometimes, when the breeze was right, she'd lie in the field and listen to it sway through the trees and bend the grass back and forth. She'd feel the warmth of the sun wash over her as she closed her eyes and smiled.

At night, she slept alone in the dark. Sometimes she'd sleep in her children's old beds, the many faces on the posters that covered the wall seeming dark and eerie in the night. Old guardians that seemed to stare down at her as she slept.

Her heart would race when the phone rang. She'd often spend most of her morning sitting by the phone, waiting for it to ring. More often than not it was someone trying to sell her something. But sometimes it was one of her children. Her daughter called her the most. She would call from Paris. She had moved there when she turned eighteen to become a fashion designer, and after an eleven-year career she'd finally reached the position of her dreams. The mother loved listening to her daughter talk about her life. She was proud of her, but she missed her dearly. She wouldn't dare admit it, but deep down there was a small part of her that wanted her daughter to fail. If her daughter failed it meant that she could pick up the pieces. She could be there again like she used to, and things could go back to the way they were before. She could have her daughter back, and then she wouldn't have to listen to the chiming in the wind. But just as quickly as those thoughts came she ushered them away.

Her two sons were in business together in the city. They had started up their own pool-cleaning company, which was now the leading business of its type in the state. They called her now and then, but as the years passed their visits and calls became less frequent.

Her eightieth birthday was in two days. She was looking forward to it because she knew that she'd get a flood of phone calls from relatives and friends. It was the highlight of her year.

Two days passed, and she sat on her chair next to the home phone. She wore her favourite dress and a little ribbon in her hair. She saved the dress for special occasions. She waited all morning for a call, but none came. She wondered if there was something wrong with the phone line. She tried calling the local pizza shop to see, and when they answered her call she quickly hung up. She looked over at the clock; it was a quarter past eleven, and still, no one had called.

Hours passed and there were no calls. She felt like crying, but remembered herself and swallowed the tears.

And then the wind chimes sang in the breeze. This was too much. She broke down and sobbed. Little droplets of salty tears fell on her lap, and her forearm was moist where she wiped her eyes.

She'd been forgotten.

But, at four o'clock in the afternoon, she heard a knock on her door. She rose from her chair and shuffled slowly over to the front door.

She gasped when she opened it. Her children were there, all of them. And by their legs were her grandchildren. She gasped in delight, this time her tears were from happiness, and for the rest of the day she ate, talked, and hugged her children. Her grandchildren couldn't handle any more cuddles, and they were sick of getting their cheeks pinched and kissed. At the first chance, they left the table to run around the house playing tip, or hide and seek. And all that could be heard was their yells and the sound of their little feet running across the floors.

Wandering far and wide

Over mountains and under trees

You try to find yourself within the vibration

Of waves that all blend into one

You wonder what it's all for

But every time you get close the answer changes

You try to figure out what we are

Until you realise we are all the same

The same people

Faceless and with many faces all at once

I see them when I sleep

Or when I'm waiting at the café for my coffee

The same people

Just like me

Resigned and downcast I dissolve into the crowd full of faces

Until there is nothing at all

But a mass of swirling voices and muddled thoughts

Drifting aimlessly like a lonely cloud

On a sunny day across a blue sky

Wandering far and wide.

Mr. Adams was a middle-aged man who was lost in a fashion and way of life that was much older than he was. He prided himself on his bowler hat, his tidy moustache, and his vast knowledge of ancient and modern history. He was a man of high class, chivalry, and absolute delusion. Most of us are a little delusional. We make exceptions for ourselves or place ourselves upon pedestals that either don't exist or are clearly beyond us. Mr. Adams was on the highest pedestal he could find. He basked in the glory of his knowledge, but refused to share it or pass it down to anyone else for fear that they would steal his ideas for themselves. He distrusted other men, and women even more. If there was one word that could describe Mr. Adams entirely, it was that he was lonely.

Most people felt bad for him and mistook him for a shy and well-meaning man, and so defended him and his behaviour.

When the news went around about his unexpected death, the university held a minute of silence. But after that life returned to normal, and very quickly the memory of Mr. Adams was lost forever.

Mr. Adams opened his eyes and looked around. He was lying at the foot of an enormous gate made of pearls and sleek plates of gold. There was a security guard in front of the gate holding a clipboard. He was looking down at Mr. Adams with an air of impatience. Mr. Adams got to his feet and dusted himself off. He knew where he was. He was at the gates of heaven. A great rush of excitement flooded through him as he walked towards the gate, but the guard blocked his path.

"Mr. Adams?" he said, eyeing him up and down distrustfully.

Mr. Adams nodded enthusiastically, almost pleadingly as he held his bowler hat in his hands. It was a fine bowler as well. His sister had given it to him after he published his fourth work of essays for the university. The title was a work on anthropology and it earned him quite a prestigious award. He had always loved studying humans, but he hated them with a passion. He hated their dirtiness and their unpredictability. He hated how they talked and how they walked. How they were cursed to shit and piss multiple times a day.

The guard eyed the long list in his hand lazily, and after a few moments of careless scanning, he shook his head. "Not on the list…"

"There must be a mistake!" Mr. Adams insisted.

"No mistake, buddy…" said the guard.

"But… this is just ridiculous!" replied Mr. Adams, frustrated; he had no idea why he wasn't allowed in.

The guard shrugged. "I don't make the rules, champ…"

Mr. Adams leaned his head on one side and tried to get a glimpse behind the gate, but the guard shuffled over and stood in the way.

Frustrated and out of luck, Mr. Adams turned around and walked down the stairs miserably, disappearing into the red glow below. The lights faded suddenly, and the crowd that had formed behind the gates erupted with applause and laughter.

And the gates of heaven shut forever behind him.

LOVE AND RAGE

The ocean is a mixture of beauty and ugliness, love and rage, calmness and unpredictability. There are times when I lie on my back and watch the clouds float in the sky, lost in memories. Sometimes I dive down as deep as I can and I wait there and listen. It's a strange place, being underwater. Suddenly I can't see anything, but I can hear. I hear the little pulses of waves and the salt and sand crackling and shifting in my ears. And sometimes I can hear whales singing to one another in the darkness. I wonder what they sing about, on their lonely journeys across the sea. I can't imagine what it would be like, swimming through the deep for so many years that barnacles make a home on my body. I wonder what they think about. When they hear the song of their kind, beckoning them from the distance. The sound of sweet familiarity in a sea that's so vast and unknowable.

Some days when I'm in the ocean, it churns and rages and tries to pull me beneath the water. The ocean is the only place in the world where I've felt alive and close to death at the same time. When I was sixteen I paddled out in a storm swell. It was a stupid decision; no one was surfing and I was way over my head. I didn't even catch a wave. The current was so strong that it sucked me around the headland. I'll never forget the feeling of knowing I felt in my stomach when I looked at the wave coming towards me. I knew that I was going to die. That wave obliterated me when it landed on me. It snapped my surfboard in half and sealed my fate. Two more waves of the same size landed, and I kept telling myself over and over again to not panic. I started to take in water, my face just above the surface. The ocean was so stormy that I could barely keep afloat. I remember I was thinking about what the headline of the newspaper article about me would say the next day: "16-year-old boy dies surfing," or something to that effect. That was the only time in my life where I've told myself that I was going to die. I thought about the new school I was meant to go to the following week, and that I'd never see or experience it. I thought about my brother. My life was completely in the hands of nature; I had no control and couldn't fight against it.

But as the water pulled back from the cliff face, by instinct I grabbed a hold of the rock shelf that had revealed itself beneath me. I clambered on top of it just as the water surged back towards the cliff, and it launched me up to the rocks and out of the ocean. My legs were trembling as I clambered into the beach pool as fast as I could, and to my surprise, I hadn't been cut up by the rocks at all.

After that day, I never underestimated the sea.

MEMORIES

Harry was looking at them from his seat in the back. He was eight years old and on his way to school. Heavyset clouds brooded in the sky, and as a result, the morning was dark and dreary. The air was still and empty as if it had been rushed out by the weight of the coming storm. He wound down the window and leaned as close to it as he could, the wind pushing his hair back as he felt the cool, moist breeze against his forehead and in his eyelids. The air was filled with the smell of rain. It was a sweet smell and one that brought him a strange sense of comfort.

He was sitting at his desk when the storm hit. Great rushes of rolling thunder echoed far off in the distance, and everyone in his class stopped their work and listened. It wasn't just his class either. People in offices and on building sites stopped what they were doing and listened. The animals in the forest felt the storm on their skin and made for shelter, their hair prickling at the sound of the calling thunder. For a few moments, all was silent and still. And then, after one big inhale, the wind rushed out and rattled windows. It seeped through the gaps in doorframes and blew signs down. It whipped people's hair over their faces as they scrambled to get indoors. The boys on the building site dropped their tools and battled to secure a tarp around the open spaces of the job site, although they were secretly happy about the bad weather. One of the bricklayers, called Bobby, said that the storm would give him a chance to head home and sort out some of the long lists of errands he had, but everyone knew he was kidding himself.

The people in the offices turned and went back to work, but soon even the ceaseless sound of tapping keys that normally filled the rooms was drowned out by the roar of heavy rain.

Cars on the road pulled over and put their hazard lights on. New couples screamed with laughter as they ran together, bent over under their jackets, drenched in rain and thinking the turn of events a romantic twist to their day out. Old couples ran together as well, but they cursed one another for forgetting to bring an umbrella.

Heavy rain fell for the rest of the day, and for most of the night too. People rugged up and made themselves cosy, and everyone felt grateful to be inside. Harry was in bed too, listening to the rain against his window. He was struggling to keep his eyes open, and soon he lost the battle and fell asleep. His mum came into the room and kissed him on the forehead before she turned the light off and walked out.

And as years passed by and he grew up, he was always happy whenever storms came. They reminded him of a time when he didn't have anything on his mind except for the sound of rain and thunder.

DEATH BY ROUTINE

When we get sucked up by routine our lives flash by. Suddenly everything falls into place. The bus comes at ten to seven and your seat is always empty. You ride it to work and watch the world go by out the window. That girl gets on the bus and you meet eyes for a moment like you do every morning. But you never say hello or even smile, although you think to every time. It all becomes in sync and predictable, but the combination feels safe and comfortable.

The bus arrives and everyone gets off, the girl takes the stairs down to the underground while you continue on to get a coffee. The barista knows your order before you say anything, but you pretend to think about it before you ask anyway.

You get to work and the day passes as it always does. The bus is cramped on the way home, and your back is sore from being hunched over in your seat.

Every day passes the same, until one day you come to and decide to make a change. For a little while, your routine is shattered and you feel alive. You start doing something that you've always wanted to do. And suddenly you feel as if your life has had a reinvigoration of purpose. One day you slip and make an excuse not to do that one thing you've been working on. A week passes by and your new burning passion becomes cold and untouched. And routine takes over once more. It comes armed with warmth and comfort and the promise that something is waiting at the end of the road. You get back on the bus and go to work. You bury yourself in your career, hoping for more money in the future and a better, more fulfilled life. Although every day you spend it on things you don't need. People you once knew well become like strangers, and so do you. You catch a glimpse of yourself in the mirror. You're not who you used to be, but you're too busy to make a change. You're married now. Your wife brought sparks of passion and love into your life, but just like all things that became routine too.

You grow old together and you're happy.

The day comes when you die, but it was always meant to be that way. The gravedigger digs your grave, just as he's done hundreds of times before. After your funeral, he fills your grave in with soil and goes home, only to return the next day to fill other graves of people consumed by routine.

MIRAGE

A lost girl was walking through a vast and empty desert. There were no clouds in the sky to offer shade and the sun was hot and unforgiving. She'd lost track of how long she had been walking, and altogether lost the reasons for why and how she got to where she was. She was raised in the forests and worshipped the earth and soil. There was a mountain far off in the horizon, zigzagging in the heat, and as the girl walked she never took her eyes off its peak. There would be water there, she thought. There would be shade under the trees that surrounded it and little cracks in the face of the mountain for her to climb into and sleep peacefully. But above all else, she wished to hear the wind rustling through the trees. For too long she had listened to the desert wind howling over the dunes and whipping sand into her face. The desert wind was harsh and bitter, lamenting over a time too long ago for recollection, when great rivers flowed through its lands. It did not bring words of courage nor of tidings from other things as the forest winds did. As the forest wind breathed through the trees it carried the songs of birds. It carried the sweet smell of fruit and running water and tree sap. The girl missed the forest dearly. But it had been such a long time since she'd walked through it that she almost wondered if her memories of it were real at all.

Some days she wondered if the mountain was real and not just a mirage. She shook her head. Her parents always taught her that life was only worth living if you believed in something. Anything else was just existence. The girl was worried about existing. She was worried that if her dream was shattered she would collapse upon the sand and wait to die. Even that would be better than just existing.

She wondered if she was only alive because she believed she was alive. Or if the heat from the sun was overbearing because she believed it to be so. She wondered what would happen if she stopped believing. Would all the land around her suddenly turn to ice and snow?

Each day that passed she walked as far as she could, and yet the mountain wasn't getting any nearer. At night, she'd lie on her back and look up at the stars in silence, wondering if her family was looking at them too. She missed them. She wondered where they were. She missed coming home from school and playing with her little sister. Or when her aunt would come over and play dress-up with her in the garden. She put her hand against her cheek and wished that she had never rubbed off the kisses that her mum had put there. She would always squirm when her mum tried to kiss her, even more so when it was in front of someone.

After those lonely nights, she awoke more determined than ever to make it out of the desert.

One afternoon, when the sun was at its highest, she came upon some footsteps in the sand and realised that she had been walking in circles. She lay down and cried, and waited there to die. She didn't believe anymore. There was no mountain and no trees. There were no bird songs and sweet, trickling streams. There was only sand, and howling, empty wind.

She lay there until the sunset, and the stars awoke in the night. But something else happened that surprised her more than the mirage of the mountain. It was that nothing happened at all.

She was still alive. She didn't believe anymore, but the world was still there. She buried her hands within the sand and felt that it was still there, and looked upon the same stars and the same moon that had been there when she did believe.

Finally, she fell asleep, exhausted from the day. The next morning, she stood up and kept walking.

I hope that one day she found the forest again.

"Excuse me, sir," started Mr. Adams, a little sheepishly, "I know this may seem like a silly question, but where am I?

"River Styx, bro. You getting on this boat or what?" replied an impatient teenager in a black hoodie.

Mr. Adams looked at the little dingy at the dock, and back to the teenager. "Can you get me back home?" he asked.

The teenager shook his head. "Nah, but I can get you to where you need to go."

"Where's that?"

"How the fuck would I know? I just paddle," replied the teenager, hopping into the dingy and motioning Mr. Adams to get in.

It was a long and quiet ride. The dingy glided over a still lake within an enormous tunnel. Mr. Adams looked up at the rocky ceiling covered in moss that glowed like stars. It was a strange and eerie place, but for some reason, Mr. Adams felt like he had been there before.

"What's your name?" Mr. Adams asked, hoping to break the tension.

The teenager rolled his eyes. "Fuck, man, here I was thinking that maybe I was about to get a ride without any smalltalk…"

Mr. Adams went to apologize but the teenager waved it off. "Nah, you're alright, man. My name's Char. I already know your name."

It took some time before Mr. Adams worked himself up enough to talk again. "Before this, I was up some stairs at another place, but the bouncer wouldn't let me through the gate."

Char laughed. "Fuck, really? That's not good. Damn, looking at you I would have thought you'd be alright. What did you do to end up here?"

Mr. Adams shook his head. "I'm sorry, I don't know what you mean?"

"Well, if you're not going there then there's only one other place you could be going," said Char.

"I thought you said you just paddled the boat?"

"Yeah… but I have a feeling."

"Where am I going?" asked Mr. Adams again.

"It's hard to say, it's different for everyone." Char stopped rowing the boat, but strangely enough, it kept gliding. "For example, I'd probably end up stuck in a room with some guy who only ever talked about the weather or some shit like that. I dunno what'd be in store for you. What do you hate the most?"

Mr. Adams's stomach dropped. "Are you telling me I'm going to Hell?"

Char shrugged. "It sounds rough when you put it like that, but yeah, I guess so…"

Mr. Adams cowered in fear at the edge of the boat. He looked over the side and considered jumping out and trying to swim back to the steps. He wondered if the bouncer would change his mind. He touched the silky water beneath the boat with his hand and recoiled in horror. A dead hand darted from the depths and just missed the cuff of Mr. Adams's jacket. Mr. Adams screamed and Char winced.

"Yeah, bro, I probably wouldn't do that if I was you, aye? And relax, man, hell's probably not as bad as you think. A guy like you is probably only gonna get some light treatment anyways."

"But I haven't done anything wrong!" said Mr. Adams.

Char raised an eyebrow. "Really? So, you've never done a single bad thing in your whole life?"

Mr. Adams stopped and searched his memories desperately for the times where he'd broken the law or done some misdoing to someone. He shuddered when he thought about all the homeless people he walked past in the city, and the one time he lied to a charity volunteer to get out of being guilt-tripped into donating. "But those are all little things... surely I don't deserve to be punished."

"I dunno, man. Little to you. A murderer could say the same thing if he finds nothing wrong with killing people."

"But I'm not a murderer!" said Mr. Adams, desperately now.

"Fuck, man, relax – I never said you were a murderer. Maybe you're going to Hell for being an insufferable little crybaby."

Mr. Adams fell silent and stared out over the water in disbelief.

A few moments later Char apologised. "Sorry, man, that was a little too much when I called you a crybaby. I guess I'm experiencing a little Hell of my own right now too."

Mr. Adams forgave him, but they didn't speak again properly for the remainder of the trip.

After what seemed an eternity, the dingy rushed up against the shore of a little island. Char hopped out of the boat and pulled it further up onto the sand.

"Well, here we go, man. I can't go any further."

Mr. Adams climbed out of the boat, still fingering his bowler hat uncertainly. "Thanks for the ride."

Char nodded as he pushed the boat back into the water and jumped in. Mr. Adams sat on the shore and watched Char float away silently before he finally disappeared into the darkness beyond.

Fear rose from the pit of Mr. Adams's stomach, and very slowly he made his way from the beach into the forest above it.

"If this is Hell, it's not so bad…" he said to himself in frail reassurance as he walked through the forest. It was desolate, but it wasn't scary. He could hear birds chirping in the trees, and, far off in the distance, he could hear the roar of an enormous waterfall.

On his way up the pathway that wound towards the waterfall, Mr. Adams was stopped in his tracks by a Sphinx. The beast eyed him up and down hungrily as it purred silkily.

Mr. Adams's legs started to quiver. He'd never liked cats.

"Uh… hello?" he said in a shaky voice.

The Sphinx lowered its head and sat upon its hind legs. "Hello, therrrre."

It never took its eyes off Mr. Adams, who was trying his best to keep his composure.

"Where am I?" he asked.

"You are in Tartarus."

"Tartarus?"

"Yess…" purred the Sphinx. "The land of the dead, the afterlife, Hell."

Mr. Adams's stomach sunk and he bowed his head. So he really was in Hell.

The Sphinx continued, smiling emptily, "But… there is a way out…"

Mr. Adams lifted his head. "Where? Please, I'll do anything…"

The Sphinx laughed. "You will learn in time, but to get any closer you must answer one question."

Mr. Adams nodded, but he was confused.

The Sphinx got up and started to pace back and forth slowly. "What animal has four legs in the morning, two legs in the afternoon, and three at night? Answer this, and you shall pass."

Mr. Adams scratched his head uncertainly. "What happens if I answer incorrectly?"

The Sphinx growled deeply, and Mr. Adams gulped. He had no idea, he'd always been terrible at riddles. He lifted his bowler from his head and wiped the sweat from his brow. He'd never even heard of an animal like that. It didn't help that the Sphinx kept eyeing him up and down hungrily.

A few minutes passed and Mr. Adams was about to crack under the pressure. The Sphinx crept towards him slowly; its tongue was out and its nostrils were flared as it breathed in the smell of Mr. Adams's sweaty skin.

"Oh, man…" said Mr. Adams, trembling.

The Sphinx stopped and looked at Mr. Adams, its face bearing an equal mix of anger and surprise.

"What's wrong?" asked Mr. Adams. If his feet hadn't felt like they were rooted to the ground then he would have run.

"You are correct."

After a moment of confusion, Mr. Adams sighed in relief, but the Sphinx was livid.

"Man. Who crawls as an infant and walks on two feet in adulthood. Who grows old and stooped and supports himself with a cane," said the Sphinx. It turned and began to walk into the forest.

"Where are you going?" Mr. Adams called after it.

"Now I must go to die…" replied the Sphinx gloomily.

"I mean… It's fine, you can just come up with another riddle – you don't have to go and kill yourself," replied Mr. Adams.

But the Sphinx ignored him and disappeared into the dense overgrowth.

Mr. Adams continued walking the path, looking up at the peak of the mountain ahead. He wondered if the way out the Sphinx was talking about was there. He didn't meet anything else along the way, but at the very peak of the mountain there stood a mirror. He looked into it and gasped; his childhood self was staring back at him. The boy looked at him with curiously worried eyes, as if he had done something wrong and was awaiting punishment. Mr. Adams knelt in front of the boy and put his hand against the mirror. The boy placed his hand against Mr. Adams's. Mr. Adams shivered – the boy's touch was cold. He looked into the boy's eyes, and suddenly he felt ashamed. That boy died a long time ago, even after Mr. Adams had promised to keep him alive.

"I'm sorry," said Mr. Adams.

The boy suddenly got shy and ran away somewhere beyond the mirror.

Mr. Adams knelt in silence for a time, reminiscing upon days long past and memories that were unchangeable and infinite.

Behind the mirror was a chasm that delved deep into the belly of the mountain. Mr. Adams could smell sulphur, and feel the immense heat as he got closer. He peered over the edge at the magma below for a moment but pulled his face quickly away from the heat. He rubbed his eyes – they burned, but luckily he wasn't blinded.

"What do you want me to do?" He looked towards the heavens, but there was no response. He knew deep down what he needed to do. He stood with his back facing the edge this time so that his eyes would be protected. He looked around one last time before he let himself fall into oblivion. He looked at the little boy, he was out of the mirror now and watching in curious silence. Mr. Adams smiled at him. "Goodbye."

Without another thought, he fell backward into the chasm.

He closed his eyes and braced himself for impact. He screamed, wriggling and crying as a pair of silicone-clad hands pulled him loose and lifted him to the light. "It's a boy!" His umbilical cord was cut and the silicone hands placed him gently into the breast of something much softer and full of love.

His mother looked over his face for the first time and sobbed with a mixture of pure joy and exhaustion.

And he was reborn.

BUSH BUD

Australia. A big island where the soil is so arid
that it grows the crustiest, flakiest bush weed.
You wouldn't even have to grind it down to
smoke it; it turns to dust as soon as you rub it
between your fingers. The weed in Australia is
the best and also the worst of the worst. It's the
best 'cus there's shitloads of it, but it's the
worst too 'cus all of its shit. The weed's sweet in
Europe and America. Grown with care in special
greenhouses and sent off across the country
like a well-run mailing business.

Australia is different. Good weed is hard
to come by, but now and then you'd stumble
across some stuff that would shwack your
fuckin' brains out. Me and the boys used to
peddle it. Every week Pez and I would drive big
loads of it down from Nimbin in the back of my
car. The smell used to wig me out hard. It's a
miracle I never got pulled over by the cops.

A lot of things that happened in my life
were miracles. I dunno why, but I never thought
I deserved them. They weren't ever big things.
To someone like you, they wouldn't have
seemed much at all. I guess maybe they were

miracles because I appreciated them as if they were.

I didn't have much growing up. It's not a sob story, but I guess I just want you to know where I'm coming from. I started smoking weed when I was thirteen – my older brother gave me my first puff one Saturday morning right before I left for rugby. By the time I was fourteen, I was smoking with my friends at the park every weekend after we surfed or skated. A couple of little shits. Now I yell at kids who are like I was. They do my head in. I guess that's life.

I remember this one time we broke into the indoor basketball courts around the corner from my house. It all went well until Pez sat on one of the buzzer buttons accidentally and set the sirens off. Fuck, we were laughing our heads off while we ran. I guess what I'm trying to get at is that weed was a part of my life. We broke into those courts partly so we could play basketball in peace, but mainly because we wanted to smoke. I bought it every week, but never in my wildest dreams did I imagine myself trafficking it in such large quantities.

I used to drive for this guy who called himself Mr. B. He always called me from different numbers and he'd say the same thing every time, "And if you think about runnin' off with it you're a fuckin' dead cunt."

I wouldn't have run off anyways, and he scared the shit out of me so much that even just the thought of running off would make my heart race. Pez reckoned Mr. B must have been a part of some bikie gang or something. There was no way a local from Nimbin could run an operation like that. I didn't think about it too much. As long as he left the payment in the bushes I took the shipment with no complaint.

Pez and I grew up with each other, we used to surf and skate every day, and at night we'd play computer games. Those were good times. Anyway, that should tell you that in all those memories of weed I told you about, Pez was right there next to me. My memories were his, and it was only natural that we became kind of business partners, shipping weed down the coast of New South Wales.

It was all going well for a couple of months. Together, Pez and I were making around two grand a week each, just from picking up and dropping off. I dunno how much Mr. B made a week, probably a fuckload if he was willing to pay two cunts like us four grand a week.

Neither Pez or I came from money, and until that time I'd always thought we were the same in most things. But money has a strange effect on people. It turned Pez crazy. While I was stashing my money away in a shoebox under my bed, Pez was blowing it every weekend on cocaine, prostitutes and pokie machines. Don't get me wrong, I did that as well, but it was a once-in-a-while type of thing. Pez started to spin out of control. He was never a violent guy, but all of sudden he was punching on with randoms every weekend. I hated fighting. The truth was I was scared; I always kind of have been. I was scared to get beaten up, even though I tried to act like I wasn't.

Pez started taking more chances. He'd risk shit that I'd never even attempt. We got pulled over by the police in Pez's car once. He waited for the cop to get out of his car and halfway towards us before he hit the gas and we busted through some back roads. We didn't even have anything on us. He was getting paranoid. That's when I knew I had to distance myself from him.

We both knew we were gonna go to prison sooner or later. Prison's no place for a guy like me. I reckon I'd be some big bikie guy's bitch in no time. I used to stay up all night watching prison documentaries. I dunno why I did it. Maybe it was my mind trying to train me up for what was to come. I knew that I'd get bagged one day as well. I wasn't a criminal, I told myself, I just liked to smoke weed. It's funny how quickly things can get out of hand. The last time I saw Pez I walked in on him smoking meth. I tried to talk to him about it. I tried to tell him that he was fucking his life up, but he wouldn't listen. He snapped and beat the shit out of me. I wanted to fight back but I couldn't; he was my friend. We never hung out after that.

What was scary was that I was starting to see myself going down the same road. It was the lowest point in my life. My family didn't want me around, and Pez was gone. I found myself hanging around the pokies a lot more. I guess a part of me wanted to bump into Pez there. Even after what had happened. I started hanging around with the same people he used to – proper cokeheads, but I guess he got too crazy even for them. They told me he started smoking shard in front of them and it got so bad they had to tell him to fuck off.

The drugs of despair. It's strange how alluring they are to a broken heart. Lost souls that are drawn towards it like a moth to light.

I was fucked, and I was getting worse quick. But I guess another one of those miracles happened to me. I fell in love. I stopped selling pretty soon after she and I were officially dating. I dunno what it was. Maybe it was because I wanted to look good in front of her, or maybe it was because somehow she made me feel more of a man than I was. Whatever it was, it completely changed my life around.

Pez never stopped, though. A couple of months later he got into a proper brawl at a pub and he put someone into a coma. He got a couple of years for that. They reckoned it was a king-hit.

I heard from someone that he found God in there. It's funny, only the people who never seem to be looking for Him find Him. In a way that was a miracle in itself, to some people I guess. I hope he's doing well anyways.

Travelling faster than the speed of light

You look back and watch yourself dying

In a field of flowers bent gently in the wind

Your last breath escapes your body and joins the universe.

Eight billion portraits

Upon a canvas made of oil

Sit out in the open

Destined one day to spoil

Eight billion portraits

Each one different from the next

Are somehow all the same

They sit cut off at the necks

Eight billion portraits

I wonder if they have names

I take a closer look at their faces

And realise all of them are in pain.

Moments in life when you come to

You look at your hands and your surroundings

And wonder how you got to where you are

You wonder why things have to be this way

And if there's any point in it all

Sooner or later you find something

A partner or someone

And suddenly your life is full of meaning

Of equal parts love and fear

Love for everything in your life

And the fear that at any moment you could lose
it all

Scattered in the wind

Like bits of debris

Fragmented memories to relive again

At night when you are alone.

I wonder if I'll die alone

Spend my last waking moments staring at my phone

Darkness swallows the room but the phone screen is bright

I fixate myself on it and all of a sudden I see the light

I fall through a sky of pixels and my stomach drops

As I land in a waiting room full of people I forgot

They all look at me with their expressionless faces

Chat bubbles float above their heads with conversations left unread

Of messages that will never make it back from the afterlife

I try to reply to them but I remember that I'm dead

Scrolling through memories of when I was alive.

The characters we create over our lives

Become a part of us, like badges on a jacket

Souvenirs from journeys long past

Wandering and wondering along the way

We come to realise we are all of them and none at all

We are no one, nowhere

Under skies much older than time itself

Lost beneath the stars.

THE BOYS

Old times and new times as well.

Memories of those times run through my head every night before I sleep. I remember them so vividly, those times when me and the boys would be running amok through the streets back home. That town was small, too small for us. There were four of us in total. Me, Johnny, Spud and Gus. We used to do mainies on our bikes every weekend, checking out the only good-looking girl in town, Alice Sprinston. Only problem was that she was going out with some lame footy player none of us liked. He was alright, but he was one of those blokes that instantly alpha'd you with his presence.

Anyways, that wasn't the only thing the four of us did. Our town was small, and surrounding it were long dusty plains as far as the eye could see. We had to make fun for ourselves. We'd fight a lot, or try and set fire to things. We'd jump off houses, or tow each other on the back of our bikes while we skateboarded. If you put four boys with ADHD out in the bush with nothing to do, what the fuck do you reckon would happen? It's a blessing none of us got too rowdy and burned the whole town down by accident or something like that.

Even though those times were often boring, I can't stop thinking about them. Riding my bike in the sun with the wind in my hair, listening to cicadas scream around me in the heat. Not a care in the world. Those memories make my life feel beautiful. I heard a poet say that beauty is equal parts pain and happiness. I reckon he's right, I feel like I've had a lot of both of those things.

I remember when we all turned eighteen and we started going to the local pub. The first time we stepped through the front door all the old boys rolled their eyes. First thing Spud did was sit at the piano and play a song. I never even knew that he could play piano. He was the dumbest cunt I'd ever met, but, man, he knew how to play the piano beautifully. I looked at him a little differently after that. He was always a quiet guy, he never gave too much of himself away. I had no idea at the time that he'd become what he did. He got married in his early twenties, but one day he came home from work and found out his wife had run off with another man. He ended up finding them both and killing them, and then he killed himself. I remember standing over his grave in silence. It's a strange feeling, knowing someone who's dead. I hadn't seen him in a few years – when we went to boarding school he and I had a falling out. It wasn't his fault, it was mine.

I'd never been around so many other kids, especially in the city, and all I wanted to do was fit in. I wanted it so bad I even sacrificed my three best friends to get there. I made friends with some of the popular guys just because I was hanging around them all the time. Eventually they started inviting me to their parties and stuff, and after that I never saw Spud, Johnny and Gus anymore. That's one of my biggest regrets. When you wanna be someone so bad you'd do anything to become like them, even lose yourself. That's what it felt like when I spent time with the popular boys. I felt too uncomfortable to be myself around them. I'd say shit that I'd normally cringe at, and I'd do things with them that normally I'd despise, but what are you gonna tell a teenage boy who's finally started hanging out with the cool kids?

I still keep in contact with Johnny and Gus. Both of them have families now, they're running their own farms and that, and it sounds like they've got good things going for them. I moved to Sydney a while back. Was just searching for something bigger, I guess. I dunno if I've found it yet, I dunno if you're ever supposed to. I hope I do. And when I do I hope it's still beautiful.

THANK YOU

When I was seventeen, my family was in a pretty bad position financially. We ended up having to move out of the place we were renting – we couldn't afford the rent for a house, and so we downsized. My sister went with my mum, and I moved into the shared house that my brother was living in.

My room was in the cupboard and I slept under an inbuilt table that had just enough room under it to fit a single mattress. I loved that place. My brother and his friends called it 'the shack'. It was a small wooden house just a few streets away from the beach. I was stoked to live there. I surfed every day after school, and me and my friends would smoke bongs there on the weekends. Every morning I'd wake up with wood chips in my eyes from the underside of the table. Besides that, it was a pretty comfy place to sleep. I'd always imagine that I was a bear in hibernation or something like that, and I'd found a little hollow in an enormous tree that'd protect me and keep me warm from the snow.

Maybe, at first glance, that situation would seem kind of heavy, but it was one of the best times of my life. I always laugh with my brother about the time I told my bosses at the café I was working at that I was sleeping under a table. They started giving me free food to take home with me, sandwiches and muffins and stuff.

That's when I started writing. When I finished school, I had a lot of anxiety about the future. I had no idea what to do with my life, and it felt like any choice I made at the time would be final. I started listening to music every night and drawing characters in a little art book I had, and then I'd write a poem about their lives. They all started off as fantasy poems, and it got to the point that I had so many characters and poems that I decided to create my own fantasy universe with them, called Elestrium. I worked on that world for years. I wrote books about it, made podcasts and drew heaps of stuff, although my drawings were awful, so I got a lot of them redrawn by a friend who was actually good at art.

Then I moved to London to work as a writer, although I ended up working at a café. I applied for a job as a junior editor at Penguin, but I made a spelling mistake in my cover letter by accident and sent it off without reading it over again. Although I probably wouldn't have got it anyways, I'm fucking awful at grammar.

London was a hard place to live with no money. I worked at a café during the day and a bar at night, but I was always broke. I ate cans of soup for dinner and hoped that a men's multivitamin would do the rest of the job.

I started writing my first book, *The White Ape*, there, and during the same period, I fell in love for the first time. Those days were beautiful, but short-lived. The relationship ended and I was shattered. It's funny looking back at it now. Heartbreak is that one universal feeling that everyone can sympathise with.

I remember reading a book about a secret library in Syria, where a bunch of university students risked their lives trying to collect books in the dead of night from the rubble of their besieged city. They'd been building a secret underground library for the people that remained there, and at the same time, they were fighting against the soldiers of the Assad government. I remember the author of the book asked one of the guys what his biggest fear was. Obviously, I expected him to say 'Getting killed on the front line' or something like that, but he said that his greatest fear was that his girlfriend would dump him while she was staying in another city. Love is the thing that connects us all, no matter where or who you are.

When I moved back from London I was depressed for what seemed a long while. I couldn't get over this girl and I felt as far away from my dream of becoming a writer as ever before. But time went on and I kept writing. I've written a couple of books now, but it'll be a long time before my dreams are realised.

If there's one thing I've learned, it's that most things in life are uncertain. Things can often take turns for the worse. But one thing that has always been with me is writing. I love disappearing into worlds that are distant and unlike our own. I'm thankful for that. And I'm thankful for all of you, who take the time out of your lives to read my stuff and venture through those worlds and scenarios with me. Being able to go on those journeys with you is a dream come true in itself and I can't thank you enough.

Thanks so much for reading *No one, Nowhere*.

More to come.

no one
nowhere
E.S. Higgins